MY COLLECTION OF
FAVOURITE TALES

Enid Blyton™

Published by
Grandreams Limited
435-437 Edgware Road, Little Venice
London W2 1TH

Printed in Malaysia

CONTENTS

Enid Blyton ™

The Talking Shoes

Once there was a little girl called Jennifer. She walked a mile to school each day and back, and that was quite a long way.

The first thing she did each morning was look out of her bedroom window to see what the weather was like. Then she could decide what to wear on the way to school. Sometimes it rained and then she took her mac. Sometimes it was cold and she took her coat – and sometimes it was very hot and she wore no coat at all, but a shady hat in case she got sunstroke.

One day she set out in the sunshine. It was a nice, sunny, autumn day. The leaves had turned a wonderful golden-brown colour. Jennifer had a short coat on, and her lace-up shoes, and her school hat. She ran along, singing a song she was learning at school. Jennifer liked school most of the time, although sometimes she wished she could be playing with her toys – instead of being stuck in a boring old classroom!

Half-way to school a great black cloud came up and it began to pour with rain. How it poured! You should have seen it. The rain came down like slanting lines of silver, and big puddles came all along the road. It rained and it rained and it rained! More and more puddles appeared and it seemed as though the rain would never stop.

Jennifer stood under a tree to shelter herself. She wished she was wearing her mac! She would be late for school if it did not stop raining soon. When the rain finally stopped she ran out into the road again – and stepped right into a most enormous puddle! It was deeper than her ankles – so she wetted her shoes and socks dreadfully. Her feet were well and truly soaked.

"Good gracious!" said Jennifer, in dismay. "Now look what I've done! I shall have to sit in school with wet shoes and socks all morning, and I shall get an awful cold." She sighed loudly. The last thing Jennifer wanted was to get a cold – being ill in bed was simply no fun at all!

She walked along very sadly, thinking of how she would sneeze and cough the next day – if she was ill she would not be able to visit her cousins at the weekend. Jennifer felt very disappointed, she had been looking forward to seeing them again. Her Aunt had promised to take them to the seaside and now she would not be able to go.

Just then she passed by a little yellow cottage where a dear old lady lived all alone.

The old lady was shaking the crumbs off her tablecloth for the birds in the garden. The birds visited the old lady each morning and were happy to eat up all her breakfast crumbs! She called to Jennifer, who knew her well. Jennifer always waved to the lady as she passed the cottage on her way to school each morning.

"Did you get caught in that rainstorm, my dear?"

"Yes, I did," said Jennifer sadly. "And just look at my shoes and socks! I stepped into a puddle, and they are wet through!"

"Dear me, that's dangerous. You could catch a nasty cold wearing wet shoes and socks," said the old woman at once. "Come along in and I'll see if I can lend you a pair of my stockings, and a dry pair of shoes. I have a very small foot, so maybe I can manage something for you."

So Jennifer went into the tidy little cottage, and the old lady found a pair of lace-up shoes for Jennifer, and a pair of stockings.

"There!" she said. "These will do nicely. I can lend you a pair of garters, too, to keep up the stockings. Put them on, my dear, and I will dry your wet things and have them ready for you by the time you pass by at dinner-time."

"Thank you for being so kind," said Jennifer. "Now I will not get a cold and I shall be able to visit my cousins at the weekend after all." She smiled a huge smile and finished the mug of warm cocoa that the old lady had made her.

Jennifer put on the stockings. Then she put on the shoes. They had big tongues to them, and long laces, but they were most comfortable. They felt nice and dry too.

"Thank you," said Jennifer gratefully. "I'll try not to tread in any more puddles with these on." She felt very pleased that she did not have to wear her horrible wet shoes and socks all morning. Jennifer was very thankful to the kind old lady for helping her out.

Jennifer skipped off to school.

The old lady stood at the gate and called after her. "Oh – Jennifer dear – just a minute. Don't be naughty at school today, will you? You may be sorry if you are!"

"How funny!" thought Jennifer. "Why should I have to be specially good today? I don't know."

She ran off down the path waving goodbye. Jennifer was puzzled by the old lady's warning to be good, but there was no time to think about that now – she must hurry or else she would be late for school!

She arrived at school just as the teacher was ringing the school bell. She raced into the classroom and slid quickly into her seat feeling rather hot and bothered as she had run all the way from the old lady's cottage.

Jennifer was not very good at school. It must be said that she was not very good at all. She whispered and talked when she shouldn't. She made a mess in her writing book instead of keeping it nice and tidy. She pulled the plaits of the little girl in front, and she pinched the boy next to her because she didn't like him. She took a pencil from the little girl sitting next to her and refused to give it back. And she would not share her reading book with anybody. So you see she really wasn't a very good child at school.

She didn't see any real reason why she should be good that day. So she didn't try. In fact, she was very naughty. Why *should* she have to be good? She picked up her number book so roughly that a page tore in half.

Then a funny thing happened. A voice spoke in the silence of the classroom – a rather deepdown, husky voice that no one had ever heard before.

"Careless girl, isn't she?" said the voice. "Did you see how she tore her number book?"

"Yes, I did," said another voice, just as deepdown and husky. "She ought to lose a mark for that. Mind you, she has been nothing but trouble since she got here."

"Who is talking?" asked the teacher, Miss Brown, looking around the class. She was trying to show the children how to work out a very difficult sum and expected them all to pay attention. "Who is talking?" she demanded again. Jennifer went red. How dare somebody talk about her like that? Who on earth could it be?

She wondered if it was the little boy next to her. She glanced at him out of the corner of her eye and pinched him slyly. A voice spoke loudly again.

"Did you see Jennifer pinch the little boy next to her? Isn't she cruel?"

"A most unkind child, there was absolutely no need for her to pinch him like that," said the second voice. "I don't think I like her. I don't think I like her at all."

"Oh! Who's talking like that about me!" cried Jennifer in a rage. "Who is saying such mean things about me?"

"It sounds like somebody on the ground," said Miss Brown, puzzled and alarmed. Everyone looked on the floor. Nobody was hiding beneath the tables or desks. Nobody had crept into the classroom. And nobody in the classroom could work out who was speaking. How strange! Whoever could it be? The teacher and the children were all extremely puzzled indeed. It was quite a mystery.

Have you guessed what it was that was talking? Perhaps you have! It was the tongues in the two borrowed shoes! They chattered away to one another, and were most surprising to hear.

"I think she has a very cross face, don't you?" said one tongue. "It's a pity she doesn't look in the mirror. Then she would see how horrid she looks when she keeps frowning. If she's not careful the wind will change and her face will be stuck like that forever!"

"Will you stop talking, whoever it is? I will not tell you again, now be quiet!" cried Miss Brown, and she rapped on her desk. By now she was getting most fed-up with the chattering voices interrupting her lesson.

The shoes held their tongues and stopped talking for a while. They were frightened of Miss Brown. But we know that those shoes could not be quiet for very long! The class settled down to write. They were copying from the blackboard. Jennifer did not try very hard. When she opened her desk to get out her pen her book slid to the floor.

"Good gracious!" said one tongue to the other. "Just look at Jennifer's dreadful writing! I have never seen such messy writing in all my life. Did you ever see anything so awful for a child of ten?

Really, she ought to be ashamed of herself."

"Poor thing! Perhaps she can't write any better," said the other tongue, flapping itself a little. "Look at that mistake! If I were the teacher, I would put Jennifer into the corner. I'd make her stay there until she had learnt to behave properly."

"Oh! Oh!" cried Jennifer, stamping her foot and bursting into tears. "I won't stand it! I won't stand it any more. Who is saying these horrid things about me? Who is it?"

"I can't imagine, Jenny," said Miss Brown. "All I can say is that the things are perfectly true! It is a shocking thing that a girl of ten should write so badly and be so untidy."

Jennifer picked up her book sulkily and put it on her desk. She felt very upset that someone was saying such nasty things about her. She still had absolutely no idea who was talking about her – who could it be? She opened her book and started copying from the blackboard once more. The shoes chatted together again.

"She's got her horrid, sulky face on now. That face really doesn't suit her at all. Isn't she a most unpleasant child? I wonder how many mistakes she will make on her next page! I am sure that *I* could write much tidier than Jennifer."

Jennifer set her teeth and made up her mind to make no mistakes at all. She concentrated and worked very hard. It was the quietest she had been all day! She wrote a really beautiful page and showed it to Miss Brown.

"Good gracious, Jennifer! I've never seen such nice writing from you before!" cried Miss Brown. "I think this is the neatest page you have ever written."

"You see, she can do it if she tries," said one shoe. "She's just too lazy to do it always."

"I'm not lazy, I'm not lazy! I'm not!" cried Jennifer, and she stamped her foot very hard indeed. That gave the shoes such a shock that they said nothing at all for a whole hour. Then it was geography, a lesson that Jennifer didn't like. After a while, she forgot all about trying to be good. She leaned over and pulled the hair of the little girl in front of her. The little girl squealed.

"Somebody pulled my hair!" she cried. She looked as though she might start to cry.

Miss Brown looked up crossly.

"Was it you, Jenny?" she asked.

"No, Miss Brown," said Jennifer untruthfully.

"Are you sure Jennifer?" asked the teacher.

"Yes, Miss Brown," replied Jennifer. "I didn't pull her hair."

"OoooooooooOOOOOH!" said one shoe to the other. "Isn't she untruthful? Really! Oooooooooh! How can she tell such lies? She is so untruthful!"

"Untruthful, cowardly and unkind," said the other shoe. "Why doesn't somebody send her to bed? She is very naughty indeed."

"I have never met such a mean little girl in all my life!" said the first shoe.

"I quite agree," replied the other shoe.

Jennifer glared round at everyone, thinking that somebody must be playing a trick on her, talking like this. But everyone was as astonished as she was.

"Who *is* talking?" cried Miss Brown, quite alarmed again. "I don't like this. I do not want any more interruptions to my class. I shall put the talkers into the corner if I hear any more."

"Fancy! She'd put us in the corner!" giggled a shoe. "Well, she'd have to put Jenny there, too, if she puts us." The shoe chuckled at his own joke.

"Perhaps we'd better not talk," said the other shoe. "I believe we are disturbing the class a little. Sh!"

So they said no more until it was time to go home. Miss Brown was able to finish the geography lesson in peace. The hometime bell rang. Then Jennifer went sulkily to the cloakroom and took down her hat and coat. She just wanted to go home. Another child got in her way, and she gave him a push that knocked him right over. He landed on the floor with a very surprised look on his face.

"Isn't she rough?" said the shoe, shocked. "Did you see her push that nice little boy right over? She gave him a very hard push! I wouldn't stand for that. If she did that to me, I'd kick her!"

"And I'd trip her up!" said the other shoe fiercely. "Horrid girl! Do you suppose anyone in the world likes her at all?"

"I expect her mother does," said the first shoe. "Mothers are funny – they always love their children even when the children are horrid and rude to them. I should think Jennifer is rude to her mother, wouldn't you?"

Jenny sat down on a bench and began to cry. "I'm *not* rude to my mother, I'm not, I'm not," she wept. "I love her. I'm kind to her. Oh, who is it saying these unkind things about me? Why are they saying such mean things? I may behave horribly sometimes, but I *can* be good when I try! I am a good girl really. I can be very good when I try!"

"I don't believe that, do you? I don't think she could be good," said one shoe.

"No," said the other. "She couldn't be good! Look at how naughty she has been today. She has caused all kinds of trouble. She's one of these spoilt children we've heard about."

The other children laughed. They were sorry for Jennifer, but they couldn't help thinking that it would do her good to hear these things. She went off crying bitterly, puzzled and unhappy.

The shoes talked on and on. They chatted about Jenny's bad writing and her wrong sums and her pinching and pushing. They chatted about how she had pulled the little girl's hair and how she had pushed the boy over in the cloak-room. They talked about how selfish they thought Jennifer was for not sharing her reading book. The shoes just kept on chattering. The faster she walked, the louder the shoes talked. Jenny sobbed and cried all the way to the little yellow cottage. The old lady was waiting for her at the gate. Jennifer hurried towards her.

"Dear, dear!" she said, when she saw Jenny coming along with red eyes and tear-stained cheeks. "What's the matter? Have those shoes been wagging their tongues too much?"

"Shoes? Wagging their tongues?" said Jenny in amazement. "What do you mean?"

"Well, those shoes I lent you this morning can be most tiresome," said the old lady. "You get used to them after a while. They belonged to my great-grandmother, you know, and were made by a brownie, so it is said. They have tongues, of course, just as your own lace-up shoes have – but these shoe tongues can talk – and talk they do! They are real chatterboxes. They could talk away all day. I expect they gave you quite a fright when you first heard them speak! I do hope they didn't give you too much of a shock, my dear. I hope they didn't say anything unkind!"

"Oh, no, we only spoke the truth! We always speak the truth," cried the two shoe tongues together, and they flapped themselves about in the shoes. Jenny looked down in amazement. Whoever heard of talking shoes? She took off the shoes very quickly indeed. She gaped at them in astonishment.

"So they were the talkers!" she said. "The tongues of my shoes! I never would have guessed that it was the shoes who were the talkers. Wait until I tell everyone at school! They will be most surprised. I never knew shoe tongues could talk!"

"Oh, my dear, they all could at one time," said the old lady. "That is why they were called tongues, you know, because they spoke. But they did say the silliest, most tiresome things, so now very few of them are allowed to talk. It became very noisy with all the shoe tongues chattering at once. And I had never heard such nonsense! It was decided that most shoes should not be allowed to speak. I can't stop the tongues in this pair of shoes, though. That's why I called to you to be good this morning – because I knew the shoe tongues would talk about it if you were naughty. They do so love to talk about a naughty child!"

"I shan't be quite so naughty in future," said Jenny, beginning to smile. "I don't like to be thought lazy and stupid and horrid. I know that I can be really good when I try. Lend me your shoes in a month's time, and see if they can say heaps of nice things about me for a change, will you? I will be good at school. I will listen to Miss Brown when she is talking and I shall make sure that my school books are neat and tidy. I will be kind to the other children in my class and I shan't be naughty at all! Please can I borrow the shoes in a month?"

"Certainly," said the old lady, slipping Jenny's own shoes on her feet. "How cross they will be if there is nothing naughty they can chat about! Those shoes become very grumpy indeed if they have nothing to talk about."

"I will call at your cottage on my way to school in a month," said Jennifer. "I will show those shoes that I can be very good. They will get a surprise!"

Jennifer said goodbye to the friendly old lady and walked home.

I'd like to hear what they say in a month's time, wouldn't you? What would your shoe tongues say if they could speak, I wonder? Do tell me!

Enid Blyton™

The Clockwork Kangaroo

The toys in Jackie's playroom were very happy together till the clockwork kangaroo came. Before the clockwork kangaroo arrived they all played together happily and there was never any trouble. The toy cupboard was a very happy place. Jackie had a big brown bear on wheels, a horse and a cart, a sailor doll, and a few other toys who lived together in the toy cupboard.

At night the sailor doll took the horse out of the cart, so that he could run free. In return the horse gave the doll a ride round the playroom. "Giddy up!" cried the sailor doll and off they went. Sometimes the horse gave the other smaller toys a ride on his back too. He loved to gallop about, and his hooves made a tiny pattering noise on the floor. Once when Jackie woke up, he heard the noise, but he thought it was the rain pattering outside! If he had looked into the playroom he would have seen that it was the horse.

The bear got the sailor doll to oil his wheels so that he could run quietly about at night without making any noise. The train didn't make much noise because it didn't run on its rails at night, but just anywhere it liked on the carpet. Sometimes the train would give the other toys a ride around the playroom. The red bouncy ball bounced all over the playroom visiting his friends. It was great fun – all the toys enjoyed their night-time adventures.

And then the jumping kangaroo came. It was a very clever toy really, because its clockwork made it jump high in the air just as a real kangaroo does. How it could jump!

"Hallo!" said the kangaroo, the first night. "How are you all? I'm a jumping kangaroo."

"Oh, really, how interesting!" said the bear politely. "We have never had a jumping kangaroo in the toy cupboard before. It sounds very exciting. How far can you jump?"

"I'll show you," said the kangaroo. He was eager to show the toys how high he could jump. "I bet you have never seen any toy jump as high as I can," boasted the clockwork kangaroo. He sprang high into the air – and landed, bang, on the bear's nose!

"Please don't do that again," said the bear crossly, shaking the kangaroo off his nose. He was rather annoyed with the clockwork kangaroo. He rubbed his sore nose with his paw. "Humph," said the big brown bear.

The kangaroo sprang high into the air once more – and this time he landed on the engine of the train with such a crash that he bent the little funnel.

"Look what you've done!" said the train angrily. "I was very proud of my funnel. Now you've spoilt it. I don't look like a real train any more!"

The kangaroo leapt about till his clockwork was run down. Now by the time he had finished leaping about the clockwork kangaroo had managed to upset nearly every single toy in Jackie's playroom. Then, because no one would wind him up, he sat in a corner and sulked. He just couldn't reach his own key with his paws, which was a very good thing.

He made friends with Sam, a tiny doll whom nobody liked very much, and Sam was always ready to wind him up. After that the toys didn't have a very good time at night, for the kangaroo was always jumping out at them from somewhere. He caused all sorts of mischief. He shouted "Boo!" at the sailor doll and made him fall over; he leapt over the horse giving the poor animal a very nasty fright, and it was just no fun at night-time any more!

"That clockwork kangaroo is causing all kinds of trouble. He really is a nuisance," said the bear rattling his four wheels crossly.

"So is Sam," said the sailor doll. "Always winding up the kangaroo so that he can jump on us. They cause all sorts of bother together."

"Last night he gave me such a scare that I tripped over and my bonnet came off," said the curly-haired doll. "This playroom is no longer a safe place to live!" She looked as though she might start to cry.

"I wish the kangaroo had never come to our playroom," said the train. "We were as happy as could be before. But things just aren't the same any longer. That jumping kangaroo must be taught a lesson!"

"Can't we get rid of him?" asked the horse. "Last night he jumped on my back and frightened me so much that I galloped three times round the playroom with him without stopping – and then he grinned and said, 'Thanks for the ride!' Horrid creature!" All of the toys, except Sam, were fed-up with the clockwork kangaroo.

"I wish he'd jump into the waste-paper basket!" said the bear. His nose was still sore from the last time the clockwork kangaroo had landed on it. And last night the kangaroo had jumped out and shouted "Boo!" so loudly that Bear had lost his balance and landed on the floor with a bump. The bear was most annoyed with the clockwork kangaroo. "If only he would jump into the waste-paper basket. That's deep – and he couldn't get out of there."

"Then he would be emptied into the dustbin the next morning and that would be the end of him," said the sailor doll. "That's an idea!"

"What do you mean?" asked the bear.

"I'll think of some plan with the waste-paper basket," said the doll. "Don't speak to me for a minute. Imagine – no clockwork kangaroo to bother us anymore!" All the toys were silent and waited eagerly to hear what the sailor doll had to say. "I'm thinking," he said.

So he thought hard – and then he grinned at the others. The sailor doll had thought up a jolly good plan. He looked round to make sure that the kangaroo was not near, and then he whispered to the others.

"Listen!" he said. "Tomorrow night we'll pretend to have a jumping-match to see who can jump the farthest. And when it comes to the kangaroo's turn to jump, we'll quickly swing out the basket – and he'll jump right into it."

"Oh, good!" said the bear. "Let's do it."

The toys decided not to tell Sam about their plan in case he told the clockwork kangaroo.

So the next night the toys all began talking about a jumping-match, and, of course, the kangaroo came along in great excitement, for he felt sure that he would be able to win the match easily. "I can jump farther than any of you toys," boasted the kangaroo. "I am sure that I will win the competition." He jumped around excitedly, eager to show the other toys how far he could jump.

"This is the jumping-off place," said the sailor doll, drawing a little line on the carpet with a piece of white chalk. "And we'll draw a white line to show where everyone jumps to – and the one who jumps the farthest shall win the prize."

"What is the prize?" asked the kangaroo at once. "I hope it is a nice prize for I am bound to jump the farthest and win."

"The prize is a chocolate," said the bear. The kangaroo was pleased. He loved chocolate and was sure that he would win the match easily.

He wanted to have his turn first. "I am sure that I shall jump the farthest out of everybody," he said. "May I go first? I know that I shall win the chocolate. Please may I go first?" he hopped about excitedly.

"No, you may not," said the bear. "Smallest ones first. Come on, Sam."

All the toys stood by the jumping-off place. "Good luck Sam!" called the curly-haired doll. Sam made his way towards the jumping-off place. He decided he was going to try and jump as far as he could.

Sam stood on the chalk-line, grinning. He jumped – quite a good jump for such a tiny doll. The bear drew a chalk-line at the spot where he landed. "Well done, Sam! That was a good try for such a small doll," said the bear. "Now you, Ball!" he called. The red ball rolled up. It bounced off the chalk-line and did a very good jump indeed. He jumped farther than Sam. The bear drew another line.

"That's fine, Ball," he said. "I believe you will win."

"No, he won't!" cried the kangaroo at once. "I can jump much farther than Ball can. Let me try now! I know that I can win this match. Let me have a go!"

"It's not your turn," said the brown bear. "Train, come on."

"It's not fair!" cried the clockwork kangaroo. "I want to go next."

"Well, I'm afraid you'll just have to wait your turn," said the brown bear firmly. "Come on Train, it's your turn. Let's see how far you can jump."

The engine ran up and stood with its front wheels on the chalk-line. It gave a puff and jumped – but it fell right over on to its side with a clatter. It was such a loud clatter that all the toys had to put their hands over their ears.

"Goodness! What a noise! That hurt my poor ears!" said the bear. "That wasn't a very good jump, Engine. I do hope you're not hurt. Have you hurt yourself?"

"No," said the engine, and ran off into a corner on its six wheels to watch what was going to happen. The sailor doll jumped next – and his was a splendid jump, even better than the ball's. He looked very pleased with himself when he saw how far he had jumped. He even gave a little bow and all the other toys clapped loudly – except for you-know-who, of course! The kangaroo was so impatient to show that his jump would be even finer that he pushed everyone else out of the way and stood on the chalk-line himself, quite determined to win the prize.

"I will jump farther than Sam and Ball and even the sailor doll," he boasted. "I will jump farther than I have ever jumped before! I will jump right over to the other side of the playroom," said the clockwork kangaroo. "This will be the best jump of my entire life!" He got ready to jump.

"Now's the time to catch him!" whispered the bear to the sailor doll. "Where's the waste-paper basket?"

"I've got it ready under the table," whispered back the doll. "I'll go and push it out just as the kangaroo jumps! Don't say 'one, two, three, jump' till I'm ready. Hold on a moment." They got ready to put their plan into action.

The sailor doll ran under the table to the tall waste-paper basket. He took hold of it, ready to push it out.

"Hurry up," called the kangaroo impatiently. "We prize jumpers cannot wait around all day, you know!"

The bear saw that the sailor doll was ready and counted for the kangaroo. "Are you ready? Now, one, two, three, JUMP!"

The kangaroo jumped. My, he did jump well! The doll saw him sailing through the air as if he had wings – and then with a hard push the waste-paper basket was set right under the kangaroo – and he fell into it, plomp!

He was most surprised. He sat down on some apple-peel and torn-up paper and blinked his eyes in astonishment.

"What's this?" he thought. "What's this?" He could not work out where he had landed. It was quite dark where he was and there was a most peculiar smell.

"Got him!" said the sailor doll in delight. All the toys danced round the basket in joy, except Sam, and he was cross. But he couldn't do anything at all. He had had no idea that the toys were going to trap the clockwork kangaroo in the waste-paper basket. But there was nothing he could do to help his friend.

He sat down in the corner of the playroom feeling rather annoyed.

The toys carried on dancing around the waste-paper basket. "No more jumping kangaroo," cried the bear.

"What a clever idea of mine it was!" said the sailor doll. Just then they heard a voice coming from the waste-paper basket.

"I say! I say, can anybody hear me? I do believe that I've fallen into the waste-paper basket," called the kangaroo, trying to scramble out. "This is most extraordinary. Most extraordinary indeed."

"Yes, isn't it," giggled the sailor doll. "Didn't you see it there?"

"No, I didn't," said the kangaroo, puzzled. "It just seemed to come underneath me. I was jumping through the air and suddenly I landed in the basket. I say, help me out, somebody."

But nobody did. Sam was too small to help, and the others wouldn't even try. They thought that the clockwork kangaroo should be taught a lesson for frightening them all those times.

The kangaroo tried to jump out. He leapt higher and higher – but the basket was tall and he just couldn't jump over the top. He began to get frightened.

"My clockwork is nearly run down," he cried. "Please help me out. I can't jump over the top. I don't want to be stuck in the waste-paper basket. It is not very nice in here, you know. I hate being mixed up with apple-peel, and paper, and dead flowers."

"Serves you right," said the bear gruffly. "You are a nuisance – and the right place for nuisances is the waste-paper basket or the dustbin."

The kangaroo began to cry. His clockwork had now run down and he could jump no more. He smelt of apple-peel. He was very unhappy because he knew that the basket was emptied into the dustbin every morning. "I shall be taken away with the rubbish!" he sobbed. He started to cry even louder than before.

He began to scramble round and round the basket, like a goldfish swimming round a bowl. The toys giggled. The kangaroo had often frightened them – and now he was frightened himself. He would know what a horrid feeling it was.

Sam felt sorry for his friend, but he couldn't do anything to help him. He was a very small doll and the waste-paper basket was much bigger than him. "Oh, Kangy, I think the other toys have done this on purpose," he said sadly. "They have punished you for being naughty to them."

Well, the night went on, and the morning came – and Jane came to clean the playroom. She carried away the basket to empty it into the dustbin. And then the toys began to feel rather dreadful. They started to feel very sorry for the clockwork kangaroo.

"Oh dear, what have we done to poor old Kangaroo?" said the curly-haired doll.

"I don't much like to think of Kangaroo in the smelly old dustbin," said the sailor doll. "What happens to things in the dustbin?"

"I don't know," said the bear. "I hope he is all right. Do you think he is very unhappy?"

Certainly the kangaroo was *most* unhappy. Jane had emptied him into the dustbin, and he had fallen on to a pile of wet tea-leaves, which stuck all over him. It was very uncomfortable in the dustbin, and it was much darker than the waste-paper basket.

"I must try and get out of here," said the kangaroo. "If only I could get out I would never scare the toys ever again." He sighed very loudly.

"If only I had just one more jump left!" sighed the kangaroo sadly. "I am sure that if I had just one more jump I would be able to leap out. The next time anyone takes the lid off the dustbin I could jump out, for I am near the top. I wish I had just one more jump left."

Just as he spoke, Jane came to put some cinders there. She took off the lid and emptied the pan of cinders all over the kangaroo. He gathered himself together and did one last jump. Out he leapt – and Jane gave a yell. He gave her quite a shock.

"My gracious! What's this leaping about? What on earth could it be?"

She bent down and picked up the kangaroo. "Well, if it isn't the clockwork kangaroo. I wonder what he is doing in the dustbin. He must have got in here by mistake. I'll take him back to the playroom. What a state he is in!"

She took him back. Jackie wasn't there, so she put the dirty, cindery toy on the floor and left him there. He groaned, and the toys peeped out at him. At first they didn't know who it was, for the kangaroo was so dirty and so spotted with tea-leaves. He looked extremely different from the clockwork kangaroo that they had last seen. "Who on earth could that be?" asked the sailor doll.

"I don't recognise him," said the bear. "He is very dirty whoever he is."

"Toys!" groaned the kangaroo. "Help me. I'm sorry I ever annoyed you. Do, do help me."

"Oh my goodness!" exclaimed the bear. "It's Kangaroo!"

The toys were so pleased to think that the kangaroo was back that they all rushed to help him.

They washed him. They brushed him. In fact, they couldn't do enough for him, and he almost cried for joy.

"It was dreadful in the dustbin," he said. "Really dreadful. Don't send me there any more. I'll never behave so badly again."

"Well, perhaps we've behaved badly too," said the sailor doll, ashamed. "We're terribly sorry that you ended up in the dustbin. We didn't mean to frighten you so much. You be kind to us, Kangaroo, and we'll be kind to you. There's nothing like kindness, you know."

Now the kangaroo never leaps on anyone, but instead he gives the sailor doll and Sam piggy-backs when he jumps – which is really *most* exciting for them. Didn't he have a horrid adventure? The toy cupboard is once again a happy place to live. And the toys have all sorts of exciting adventures after Jackie has put them away for the night!

Enid Blyton™

WANTED –
A Hot Water Bottle

One night, when the toys were talking quietly together in the nursery, keeping close to one another because it was very cold, and the fire was almost out, they heard an excited voice outside the window.

"Hey! Let me in! Quick!" Then there was an impatient tapping on the pane. "Hurry! It's cold out here!"

The dog jumped up. "It sounds like Little-Feet, the brownie," he said. "I'll let him in." He went over to the window and sure enough there was Little-Feet waving at him through the glass.

"Hallo!" he called. "Hurry, Dog, you must let me in!"

"Hang on," called the dog.

He pushed up the window a little and the brownie hopped in. "Thank you, Dog, I thought I was going to be stuck out there all night! I say, there are twelve tiny pixies outside in the cold," he said excitedly. "They are as small as the dolls'-house dolls. They were going along in a rabbit-carriage when a wheel came off. Luckily, nobody was hurt – except for the rabbit-carriage of course!"

"I'm glad nobody was hurt. Is it being mended?" said the teddy bear.

"Yes, my brownie friend is mending their carriage for them. He is the best brownie mechanic in the land! I am sure he will be able to fix it. He is working as fast as he can. But the pixies are simply freezing," said the brownie, and his eyes darted round the nursery.

"Have you got any little hot-water bottles? I said I'd bring them some to hold, so that they wouldn't feel so cold. Have the dolls'-house dolls got any? They would be the perfect size for the pixies."

"No," said the dog. "None of us has got hot-water bottles. We just cuddle up together when the fire goes out. Sometimes we all squeeze into the big dolls' bed and sleep there."

"Well, what am I to do for those poor little pixies? They are absolutely freezing. It is so cold

outside, some pixies even have icicles hanging off their noses!" said the brownie anxiously. "I told them I'd bring them something to make them warm. Have you any hot milk?"

"No," said the bear. "Not a drop, cold or hot. Anne and Michael drank it all up for their supper. Their mother always gives them a mug of hot milk and some biscuits for their supper."

The bear, the dog, the brownie and the other toys sat and looked at one another. They

54

didn't know what to do. The brownie got cross. "Don't sit and stare. Think of something. I tell you those poor little pixies are freezing. I can't let them down. I have promised to help them and brownies must never break their promises!"

"Well," said the dog, an idea suddenly coming into his head, "perhaps Anne would let us have her hot-water bottle. She usually takes one to bed with her. It's got a nice warm cover on it. If Anne would lend it to you for the pixies

they could creep under the cover and sit on the nice warm bottle."

"Oooh, yes, then they would have a shelter over their heads, and something warm at their feet!" said the bear. "I'm sure Anne would lend us her bottle. If not, Michael would. I'll go and ask."

"That sounds like an excellent idea," said the brownie. "A hot-water bottle should do the trick. Well done, dog! Please hurry along bear – we must get the hot-water bottle to the pixies as soon as we can."

The bear slipped off to Anne's room. He tiptoed into the room as he didn't want to give Anne a fright by waking her suddenly. Anne was asleep. She was holding the warm hot-water bottle tightly to her tummy.

The bear slid his hands under the blankets and felt about for the bottle. He found it at last. It felt lovely and warm.

"Anne!" whispered the bear, climbing up on to the bed. "Anne. Do wake up. Can I borrow your hot-water bottle?" But Anne was fast asleep. He tugged at the bedclothes. "Anne," he whispered again, a little more loudly this time. "Anne, please wake up! I need your help. Do wake up!"

Anne stirred. The bear pressed himself in his middle so that he growled. He knew Anne would know who he was then. "Grrrrrrrr!"

Anne woke right up. She sat up and felt around for the bear. "Hallo, Bear. Why are you here?" she said surprised. "I thought I left you in the nursery. I didn't bring you to bed with me."

"No. I know," said the bear, holding on to Anne's arm. "Listen, Anne. I need to ask a favour. Will you lend me your hot-water bottle for a little while?"

"Whatever for?" said Anne. "Are you so cold? Cuddle down in bed with me. It is rather chilly tonight – why don't you climb into bed with me?" She picked him up and lifted him onto the bed.

"Are you very cold?" she asked the bear.

"No, I'm not cold," said the bear, "but there are a lot of little pixies outside in the garden, very cold indeed, waiting while their rabbit-carriage gets mended – and we thought if they could cuddle against your bottle it would keep them warm."

"Oh – I really must go and see them," said Anne, excited. "Imagine – pixies in my garden! I simply must go and see them!"

"No, you can't," said the bear. "It's far too cold. It is freezing outside and you are only wearing your nightclothes. I am afraid that you may catch a cold. Just hand me out your bottle, there's a kind girl. I am sure that the pixies will be ever so grateful to you."

Anne slid out her warm bottle. "Of course you may borrow my hot-water bottle," said Anne. "I hope that the pixies will be warm soon."

"Thank you," said the bear, staggering off with it, for it was as big as he was. "Go to sleep again, Anne. I'll bring the bottle back."

He took the bottle into the nursery. The toys came running up and felt it. How lovely and warm!

"Here you are, brownie," said the bear. "Anne didn't mind a bit. She was very pleased that she was able to help us out. Take it to the pixies – but for goodness' sake bring it back when the carriage is mended. It is a very nice hot-water bottle, made of red rubber. I told Anne that I would return it to her as soon as I could."

"It feels very warm," said the toy soldier. "I am sure that those pixies will be warm in no time at all. It really is very kind of Anne to lend us her hot-water bottle."

"The cover is nice too," said the dog, looking at it. "Blue, with red spots. Don't get it dirty, brownie."

"No, I won't," said the brownie, pleased at having the bottle. "I shall take very good care of it, and I am sure that the pixies will too. They will be ever so pleased. It was a terrific idea, well done everyone! Well, I'll be back soon. Good-bye."

He slid out of the window with the bottle. He let it drop to the grass below, and the toys heard the soft flop it made. Then the brownie jumped down too.

"I'll be back soon," he called over his shoulder, and he hurried off to the bottom of the garden where the pixies were waiting.

The pixies were all standing together, freezing, watching another brownie mending their broken carriage wheel.

"Phew!" said Little-Feet's brownie friend. "This is hard work. I should have your rabbit-carriage back on the road in no time at all though."

"We hope so!" cried one of the pixies. They were all huddled together and they were shivering.

"Brrr! My teeth won't stop chattering," said another.

"Nor mine," cried another.

"My hands are as cold as ice," called another pixie. "I wish I had some gloves. I hope Little-Feet

hurries up!"

Just then they were surprised to see the big brownie come up, carrying a thing they had never seen before.

"What's that?" they said in their little high voices.

"A hot-water bottle," said the brownie, putting it down flat beside them. "It will soon warm you!"

The pixies ran to it. They felt the warmth coming out of it and they cried out for joy.

"I'll lift up the cover and you can get underneath," said the brownie, lifting up the blue cover. "Go on – get under it – you are quite small enough."

So the tiny pixies all crept in between the cover and the rubber bottle. They sat down. Oooh! How deliciously warm it was. Now they wouldn't feel a bit cold. "My feet are so cold I can't feel them," said the biggest pixie. "I know what I shall do. I shall take off my shoes and put my bare feet against the warm bottle. That should soon warm them up in no time."

So she did. She unbuttoned her pair of pretty little blue shoes, with bows on the front. Then she put her cold, bare feet against the bottle, and cried out for pleasure. "Oooh, that's much better!" she exclaimed.

"Now I'm getting warm! Oh, Little-Feet the brownie, you are a clever person to find this strange warm bottle for us."

"Yes, thank you Little-Feet," cried the other pixies.

"Anne has been very kind," said the brownie. "She gave the bear her hot-water bottle straightaway.

She wanted to help you all; she is a very kind little girl."

"You must thank her for us," said the biggest pixie. "I am sure that we would have turned into blocks of ice if we had stood in the cold much longer!"

"Three cheers for Anne!" cried another pixie. "Hip pip hooray! Hip pip hooray! Hip pip hooray!" And all the pixies cheered. Then all was quiet as the pixies snuggled down onto the hot-water bottle.

The brownie mechanic was working very hard. Tip-tap, cling, clang! The wheel of the carriage was mended at last. Half the pixies were asleep on the hot-water bottle by that time! The brownie had pulled the warm cover over them all, and they felt as if they were in bed.

"Hey, pixies! Your carriage is ready!" cried the brownie who had mended it. "I've put the rabbit in the shafts for you. He is ready to take you on your way."

The pixies woke up with a jump. They crawled out of the warm, cosy place, wishing they could stay there. "How lovely and warm I feel," yawned one pixie, rubbing his eyes sleepily. "What a pity that we have to leave!" One by one the pixies woke up and clambered into the rabbit-carriage. The biggest pixie of all didn't wake up.

"Where's Bright-Eyes?" said the pixies, looking round. "Where is she? Bright-Eyes, hurry, or we shall go without you."

Bright-Eyes, the biggest pixie, woke up in a hurry. She had been having a lovely dream. She looked around and was alarmed to see that all the other pixies had disappeared. She was afraid of being left behind, and she jumped from the hot-water bottle quickly. She forgot she had taken off her shoes. She took her place in the carriage, yawning, and

then off went the rabbit at top speed, glad to be away again.

"I'll take this hot-water bottle back again now," said Little-Feet, to the other brownie. "Then we'll go to my house and have a drink of hot cocoa. I'm cold."

"That sounds good," said the brownie mechanic.

"You did a fine job on the rabbit-carriage," said Little-Feet. "I am sure that the pixies were pleased that the best mechanic in town was on hand to help! Now I must return this hot-water bottle, and then we will go home."

He went up to the nursery window. It was still open. The toys were all curled up together in the big dolls' bed, trying to keep warm. It was one of the coldest nights of the year. The toys huddled closer together. The teddy bear got out when he heard Little-Feet coming in.

"Here's the bottle, and many thanks for getting it," said Little-Feet. "It's not so hot as it was – but my word, how those pixies enjoyed the warmth. They went to sleep between the cover and the bottle! They have asked me to pass on their thanks and good wishes to Anne. All the pixies agreed that she is a most kind-hearted little girl."

"I'll slip it into Anne's bed," said the bear. "I won't wake her up again."

He dragged it over the floor and went into Anne's room. It was difficult to get it on the bed, and made him pant and puff.

Anne was fast asleep and didn't hear a thing as the bear tiptoed quietly into the room. He pulled back the covers and slid the bottle under them. Then he went back to the nursery and climbed into the dolls' bed to get warm.

Anne didn't wake when the bottle was put into her bed. All the excitement earlier had made her very tired. She slept till the morning. Her bottle was quite cold by then. She felt it against her bare leg.

She tried to remember what had happened about the bottle in the night. Of course – the bear had come to her – and borrowed her bottle to warm some pixies! Yes, that's right. How could she have forgotten such an adventure? The bear had taken the hot-water bottle

to the pixies at the bottom of the garden. Poor little things – they must have been so cold! Just wait until she told her brother!

Anne called loudly to Michael, who slept in the next room. "Michael! Michael, wake up! I have something very exciting to tell you. You'll never guess what happened! I had an adventure in the night!"

"What was it?" said Michael sleepily. He wondered why his sister sounded so excited. "Tell me what happened," he called.

"Why, the teddy bear came, and borrowed my hot-water bottle for some little pixies to warm themselves with," said Anne. "They were stuck at the bottom of our garden because their rabbit-carriage had broken-down. The poor things were freezing and so I gave the teddy bear my hot-water bottle. And he must have brought it back, because it's here again this morning."

"Anne! You know you dreamt it!" said Michael at once. "You know you did. I know that pixies do not exist. And there are definitely no pixies at the bottom of our garden! You must have dreamt it."

"I didn't," said Anne. "I remember it as well as anything."

"I remember dreams as well as anything," said Michael. "Mummy – do you know what Anne says? Tell her, Anne."

68

Anne told Mummy and Mummy laughed, too. "A nice little dream!" she said. "That's all it was!"

Anne began to feel it must have been a dream, and she was rather sad about it. She didn't want it to be a dream, she wanted it to be true. It would be so exciting if there really were pixies at the bottom of the garden.

Mummy took her bottle and Michael's, and emptied them. "I think I'll wash the covers," she said. "Yours looks quite dirty, Anne!"

She took off the covers – and then she gave a cry of surprise. In Anne's cover was a pair of shoes, dear little blue ones, with bows on the front. They were the ones Bright-Eyes had taken off, and had left behind in her hurry.

"Anne! You've been putting your doll's shoes in your hot-water bottle cover!" she said. "What a funny thing to do! I've never seen these shoes before. Where did you get them? They are the tiniest shoes I have ever seen. Did you buy them for your doll with your pocket money?" asked Mummy.

"I've never seen them before, either! I did not buy them," said Anne, in excitement.

"How strange! My, this is quite a mystery! They are so dainty. Where on earth have those shoes come from?" asked Mummy.

"I think I know," smiled Anne. "Look, Michael! Proper little pixie shoes! One of the pixies must have taken them off, and left them in my hot-water bottle cover last night. *Now* do you believe me when I say the bear came and borrowed my bottle? I told you he took the bottle to warm the pixies at the bottom of the garden!"

Well, of course, Michael had to believe Anne after that. Anne put the shoes on the feet of her biggest dolls'-house doll, and they fitted her perfectly.

"Aren't they sweet? What lovely little bows. They look so pretty with dolly's red dress," said Anne. "They are a perfect fit. I do hope the pixie won't come back for them!"

She hasn't yet – but I think Anne would be rather pleased to see her, if she did!

Enid Blyton™

The Magic
Treacle Jug

Now once when Miggle the goblin was walking home at night through Goblin Village he saw a light in Mother Tick-Tock's cottage window. He stopped and thought for a moment.

"I think I'll go and peep in," he said to himself. "Mother Tick-Tock's grandfather was a wizard, and it's said that she knows plenty of useful spells. I might see something interesting if I go and peep." Miggle was very well known in Goblin Village for his nosy ways. He just could not resist creeping up garden paths and peeping through people's windows. "What a cunning fellow you are!" said Miggle to himself. "I am bound to see something exciting at Mother Tick-Tock's house."

So he crept into the front garden and peeped in at the lighted window. Mother Tick-Tock was there, cutting large slices of bread, one after the other.

"I suppose those are for her children's supper," thought Miggle, counting them. "One, two, three, four, five, six, seven – yes, they are. Goodness me – does she give them just dry bread for their suppers, poor things? I thought that Mother Tick-Tock was a very kind lady. I am sure that she must feed her children more than just dry bread."

He watched carefully. He saw Mother Tick-Tock take up a small blue jug and he heard her speak to it. "Fancy speaking to a jug! That really is odd," exclaimed Miggle. "I knew I would see something unusual if I peered through this window – how right I was! I have never heard anyone speak to a jug before. Whatever next?"

He stood on his tiptoes so that he could see right into Mother Tick-Tock's kitchen. "Well, I don't want to miss anything!" thought Miggle. "This is ever so exciting."

His eyes were as big as saucers. Then he pressed his ear very close to the window so he could hear what Mother Tick-Tock was saying to the jug.

"Pour me treacle,
         strong and sweet,
For a Very Special Treat!"
And, to Miggle's surprise, the jug left Mother Tick-Tock's hand, poised itself above a slice of bread, and poured out good, thick, yellow treacle! Then it balanced itself above the next slice and poured more treacle. Then it went to the third slice.

"Good gracious me! How can a little jug like that hold so much treacle!" thought Miggle, in surprise. "Look at it, pouring thickly over one slice after another. Mother Tick-Tock's children will be having a tasty supper this evening. What lovely treacle too! I think that must be the finest treacle that I have ever seen. Oooh, I wish I had some of it!"

Mother Tick-Tock suddenly caught sight of Miggle's face at the window, and, leaving the jug pouring treacle on the last slice of all, she ran to the window, shouting angrily. Miggle disappeared at once and ran home at top speed. He was afraid of Mother Tick-Tock. He ran as fast as he could and he soon reached his little cottage.

But he couldn't forget that wonderful Treacle-Jug. To think of having sweet treacle at any time! Miggle loved treacle more than anything else in the world.

How lucky Mother Tick-Tock's children were. No wonder he so often saw them about with thick slices of bread and treacle. "So that's why her children always look

so happy," said Miggle. "Imagine – all that treacle!"

Now two days later Miggle made himself a fine pudding. But when he came to taste it he found that he had left out the sugar. Oooh – how horrid it was!

"Now, if only I could borrow that Treacle-Jug!" thought Miggle, longingly. "I could have treacle all

over my pudding and it would be one of the nicest I'd ever had. Treacle would make this pudding go down a treat. I wonder if Mother Tick-Tock would lend me the jug."

Just at that very moment Miggle saw someone passing his cottage, and who should it be but Mother Tick-Tock herself, on her way to visit a friend, Mrs. Know-A-Lot. Miggle knew that she went to visit Mrs. Know-A-Lot every week. Mother Tick-Tock was often gone for the best part of a day as Mrs. Know-A-Lot lived on the other side of town.

Miggle watched her go down the road, and a small thought uncurled itself in his mind.

"Couldn't I just borrow the Treacle-Jug for a few minutes? Nobody would ever know. And if it's a magic jug, the treacle would never, never come to an end, so it wouldn't matter my having just a very little! I would not need it for very long. I am sure that Mother Tick-Tock would never find out."

He sat and thought about it, looking at his sugarless pudding. He licked his lips at the thought of all that treacle. "This pudding needs treacle!" he declared. Then he popped it back into the oven to keep warm, and ran out of the front door very quickly indeed. "I must get that jug before I change my mind!" he thought. "I'll use it to cover my pudding with treacle, then I'll take it straight back. Run, Miggle, run!"

He came to Mother Tick-Tock's cottage. The door was locked, but the window was open just a crack – a big enough crack for a small goblin to put in a bony little arm and reach on to the shelf for a small blue jug! There! He had got it. But how strange – it was quite empty!

"I'd better not go too fast with it, in case I fall and break it," he thought. "I would be in such trouble if I broke the jug!" So he put it under his coat and walked back slowly. He felt very excited indeed. He couldn't wait to get home and tuck into his delicious pudding. He patted the Treacle-Jug under his coat and carried on his way.

It did not take Miggle long to reach his little cottage. He thought about treacle pudding all the way home and he was ever so careful to make sure that the jug came to no harm! He stood the blue jug on his table and fetched his pudding from the oven. "Ha, pudding – you're going to taste very nice in a minute!" he said, and set it down in the middle of his table. He picked up the jug and spoke to it solemnly, just as Mother Tick-Tock had.

"Pour me treacle,
    strong and sweet,

For a Very Special Treat!" said Miggle. The little jug left his hand at once and poised itself over the pudding. It tilted – and to Miggle's great delight a stream of rich golden treacle poured out and fell on his pudding. Miggle's mouth began to water. Oooh! That pudding was going to taste very, very nice! Very nice indeed. The pudding smelt delicious. What a clever goblin he was. Surely he was the cleverest goblin in Goblin Village! "Treacle pudding here I come!" cried Miggle gleefully.

"There! That's enough, thank you, little Treacle-Jug," said Miggle at last, smacking his lips together. His mouth started to water again when he thought about how good the pudding was going to taste. Miggle did so love treacle!

"That's perfect, I am sure it will taste delicious. Don't pour any more, or the treacle will spill out of the dish." But the jug took no notice at all. It went on pouring steadily and Miggle saw that the treacle was now dripping over the edges of the pudding-dish. "Hey! Didn't you hear what I said!" he cried. "Stop, jug!

You'll ruin my tablecloth!"

But the jug didn't stop. It still hung there in the air, treacle pouring from its little spout. And by this time, there was a thick coat of treacle all over his table. In fact, the tablecloth was disappearing quickly beneath the steady stream of treacle.

Miggle was angry. "Hey! I said stop!" he shouted. "That's my best tablecloth! I'll never get that clean. I shall probably have to buy a new one!" He snatched at the jug, but it hopped away in the air and went on pouring in another place.

"Stop, jug! Don't pour treacle into my armchair!" shouted Miggle. "Oh my goodness, look what you've done! Emptied treacle all over the seat of my chair and the cushion! Come away from there!"

Miggle chased after the Treacle-Jug. "I command that you stop pouring treacle," he bellowed. By now the little goblin had turned quite red in the face. He

snatched at the jug again, but it wouldn't let itself be caught. It got away from his grabbing hand just in time and hung itself up in the air just above the wash-tub, which was full of Miggle's dirty clothes, soaking in the suds there.

"Hey!" cried Miggle in alarm. "Not over my washing, for goodness' sake! Stop, I say! Don't you see what you're doing? You're

not supposed to pour treacle over chairs and wash-tubs, only over puddings and tarts. Oh, you mischievous jug! Wait till I get you! I'll break you in half!"

By this time poor Miggle was quite out of breath from chasing the jug around the room. "Oh, please will you stop!" he pleaded. "Look at the mess you have made. It will take me hours to clean the house. Come here!" He snatched at the jug again, but it swung away in the air and this time hung itself over the nice new hearth-rug.

"Don't you realise treacle is only supposed to be poured over food?" yelled Miggle. "It is not supposed to be poured over tables and chairs. And it is definitely not to be poured over my brand new hearth-rug!" But it was too late!

Trickle, trickle, trickle – the rich, sticky treacle poured down steadily over the rug, and poor Miggle tried to pull it away. But he soon found himself standing in treacle, for it spread gradually over the floor.

"Oooh, my poor hearth-rug!" moaned Miggle. "My poor new hearth-rug. I shall have to buy a new rug and a new tablecloth now." Poor Miggle shook his head in despair. "Even my shoes are covered in treacle. How I wish I had not taken the jug from Mother Tick-Tock's house! It is all my fault for being so greedy. Everybody is always telling me I will get into trouble one day for being so nosy – and they were right!"

Then Miggle began to feel very alarmed indeed. What was he to do with this mad Treacle-Jug? He simply MUST stop it somehow.

"Ah – I've an idea!" thought Miggle. "Where's my fishing net? I'll get that and catch the jug in it. Then I'll smash it to bits on the ground. Oh, this treacle! How I hate walking in it! It's just like glue!"

He made his way to the corner where he kept his net and took hold of it. At once the Treacle-Jug swung itself over to him and poured treacle down on his head and face. How horrible! How sticky! Miggle was so angry that he shouted at the top of his voice. I imagine the whole of Goblin Village heard Miggle as he shouted louder and louder! Miggle was an extremely angry little goblin. He started shouting at the Treacle-Jug again.

"I'll smash you! I'll break you into a hundred pieces! I'll teach you to pour treacle all over my house! You just wait!" He swung the fishing net at the jug and almost caught it. It seemed frightened and swung away out of the door and up the stairs, pouring treacle all the way. Miggle sat down and cried bitterly. His house was in a mess and most of his things were ruined. And he was covered from head to toe in sticky treacle. Whatever was he to do?

Soon he heard a curious glug-glug noise, and he looked up in alarm. A river of treacle was flowing slowly down the stairs! It flowed through the kitchen and out of the door, down the path and into the street. People passing by were quite astonished. They had never seen a river of treacle in Goblin Village

before. "It seems to be coming from Miggle's cottage," said one man. "How strange!" said his friend.

More and more people gathered to watch the treacle river flowing down the street. They stood around shaking their heads and muttering in astonishment.

Mother Tick-Tock, coming back

from visiting her friend, was astonished too. But she knew in a trice what had happened.

"Miggle's borrowed my Treacle-Jug!" she said. "I saw him peeping through the window when I used it the other night. The mean, thieving little fellow! That goblin just can't help himself; he is always getting into mischief. I knew he was up to no good when I saw him at my window."

Miggle saw Mother Tick-Tock and waded out through the treacly river to his front gate, crying, "Please, Mother Tick-Tock, I'm sorry. I can't make the jug stop pouring. Is there a spell to stop it as well as to start it?"

"Of course there is," said
Mother Tick-Tock. "It's just as well to
know both spells if you steal
something like a Treacle-Jug, Miggle.
Well, you can keep the jug if you like.
I've a much bigger one I can use.
How tired of treacle you must be,
Miggle!"

"Oh, Mother Tick-Tock, please,
please take your jug away," begged

Miggle, kneeling down in the treacle.
"My house is covered in treacle.
There is treacle all over the kitchen
table. There is treacle all over my
armchair. My new hearth-rug is
covered in treacle. I am covered in
treacle! Look, even the street is
covered in treacle. It's everywhere!
Please can you make it stop? I'll do
anything you say, if you only will!"

"Very well. If you come and dig my garden for me all the year round and keep it nice, I'll stop the jug from pouring, and take it back," said Mother Tick-Tock. Miggle groaned. He did so hate gardening! It was so boring and such hard work.

"But your garden is so big!" he exclaimed. "I shall have to spend all my time keeping your garden looking nice," moaned Miggle.

"Well, I can always leave the Treacle-Jug with you," said Mother Tick-Tock.

"No," said Miggle at once. "Please take it away. I'll come," he said. "I don't want to, but I will."

"If you don't, I'll send the jug to pour over your head," said Mother Tick-Tock, and everyone laughed. She called loudly, "Treacle-Jug, come here!"

The little blue jug sailed out of a bedroom window and hung over Miggle's head. He dodged away at once. The last thing he wanted was to get covered in more treacle!

Mother Tick-Tock chanted loudly,
"Be empty, jug,
and take yourself
Back to your place
upon my shelf!"

And – hey presto – the Treacle-Jug became quite empty, turned itself upside-down to show Mother Tick-Tock that it had obeyed her, and then flew swiftly through the air on the way to her cottage. Mother Tick-Tock knew she would find it standing quietly in its place on her kitchen-shelf.

"I will give my children bread and treacle for their supper tonight now that the Treacle-Jug has been returned to its proper home," said Mother Tick-Tock.

What's this? Miggle has turned rather a strange colour upon hearing the word 'treacle'!

Mother Tick-Tock laughed at the funny look on Miggle's face. "Well, good-bye, Miggle," she said. "You've quite a lot of cleaning up to do, haven't you? Somehow I don't think you'll want to eat treacle again in a hurry!"

She was right. Poor old Miggle can't even see a treacle-tin now without running for miles! And I'm not a bit surprised at that!

Enid Blyton ™